Lilla Dale Avery-Stuttle

Poems of the Christ Life

Arranged in a Series of Recitations for Use in Sabbath School

Lilla Dale Avery-Stuttle

Poems of the Christ Life
Arranged in a Series of Recitations for Use in Sabbath School

ISBN/EAN: 9783337408077

Printed in Europe, USA, Canada, Australia, Japan

Cover: Foto ©Andreas Hilbeck / pixelio.de

More available books at **www.hansebooks.com**

POEMS

OF THE

CHRIST LIFE,

ARRANGED IN

A Series of Recitations

FOR USE IN

SABBATH SCHOOL ENTERTAINMENTS.

BY

MRS. L. D. AVERY STUTTLE,

Author of "Satan's First Lie" and other Poems.

1893.
BEACON PUBLISHING Co., Publishers,
LANSING, MICH.

EXPLANATORY.

IN order to fully carry out the wishes of the author with reference to these poems being used as a basis of Sunday School entertainments (see author's preface), the publishers have arranged "Model Programs" for two magnificent Sunday School entertainments.

In arranging these programs great care has been exercised in selecting music which will harmonize with the recitations, so as to climax the thought of the author with the inspiring music which follows.

That every entertainment may be a flattering success in the way of attendance as well as in the excellence of the recitations, the publishers will also upon application furnish ample advertising matter for each entertainment. Many of these entertainments are already being held, and always with the utmost satisfaction to the schools and the public. As a rule, the churches are crowded from altar to vestibule, and in many instances hundreds have been unable to gain admission. The entertainment, as a whole, is a beautiful portrayal of the Christ life, in song and verse, and will certainly be of very great value to the school in calling the favorable attention of the public to Sunday School work.

BEACON PUBLISHING Co

PREFACE.

IN writing this little book, it has been the sincere wish and earnest effort of the author to so present the leading events in the life of our Divine Master as to show his wonderful love for humanity, as the main-spring of all the acts of his earth life. It is also her desire and hope that these poems may be used as the basis of a large number of Sunday School entertainments, and that in this way she may become a humble assistant to children and youth in pressing the sacred truths of the Great Teacher upon the minds and hearts of large numbers who may attend these entertainments, and receive lasting impressions for good from these young speakers.

If by reading or hearing a description of the miracles and the earth life and death of our beloved Lord, in verse form, will be the humble means in the hands of God, of leading any to love him more and to seek to become his disciple, the earnest prayer of the author will have been realized.

L. D. A. S.

BIRTH.

O'ER Bethlehem's hills the stars of night
  Were softly shining, clear and bright;
The flocks and herds were sleeping still,
On verdant dale and dewy hill,
And o'er earth's calm and peaceful breast
A benediction seemed to rest,

As though the whole creation knew,
And smiled a welcome warm and true
To Him, her long-expected Lord,   .
Foretold by Inspiration's Word,—
Foretold and sung by seer and sage,
Bright Star of Hope, from age to age.

Hark, hark! what strains of music rare,
Like faintest perfume fill the air!
And louder still, and still more loud,
Bursts from that swift descending cloud:
Such glorious notes ring o'er and o'er
As weary earth ne'er heard before;
Aloud the heavenly heralds sing,
While through the spheres the echoes ring.

"Glory to God in the highest !
   Peace and good will to men ! "
And the heavens caught the glad refrain,
   And echoed it o'er again.
Then up from the hills of glory
   There echoed the thrilling cry,
"Rejoice, O Earth, for the Christ is born !
   Glory to God on high ! "

SLAYING OF THE INNOCENTS.

THUS one by one the days go by
   Since, in the brightening orient sky,
The wise men saw the shining star
Gleam over Bethlehem's hills afar,
And since the shepherd's hearts were stirred
By sweetest song ear ever heard.

But ah ! those echoes scarce had died
O'er Judah's hills and vales so wide, —
Those hills and vales which lately flung
The echoes back from angel tongue, —
Ere, from those selfsame hills, arise
Loud wails of anguish to the skies.

O Herod ! heed'st thou not the cry
Of Rachel's anguish, rising high, —
That long, loud wail of mortal pain
From tender babes thy sword hath slain ?

Why dost thou raise thy puny arm
To do the Lord's Anointed harm?
Dost thou not know th' Eternal One
Will shield his well beloved Son?

To far-off Egypt's friendly land
He journeys, led by angel hand ;
There, safe from cruel rage, is borne,
While Rama's daughters weep and mourn.
O crafty Herod, vain thy might
When waged against Eternal Right.
Vain, vain shall be thy godless boasts,
Thy conflict with the Lord of Hosts.

IN THE TEMPLE.

O'ER Judah's plains sweet Spring had
thrown
    Her flowery robe of living green,
And Nature in her gala robes
    Was mantled like a fairy queen.

High o'er the temple's burnished towers
    The sunshine fell like molten gold,
And flamed and flashed from glittering spire,
    From pinnacle and turret old,
While through the city's busy street
Echoed the tread of countless feet.

Far over Judah's hills they come,
  From shepherd lad to stately priest,
To ancient Salem's gates they haste
  To keep the sacred Paschal Feast.

Look, who is he, that youthful Lad,
  Standing within the temple fair?
Why do not Israel's sages know
  That he — the Paschal Lamb — is there?

Strange blindness, that they knew him not,—
  Those gray haired men, those learned
    seers :
Useless the Rabbi's studied lore,
  The vain philosophy of years.

From out those sacred, youthful lips
  Flow wondrous words of heavenly lore,—
Such words of purity and grace
  As man had never heard before.

And now, a kind, obedient Son,
  No thought had he of earthly fame,
But 'mong the hills of Nazareth
  A humble carpenter became.

He took our fallen nature ; he
  Who made the hosts which roll above
Of Abraham's frail seed partook,
  In godlike sympathy and love.

THE BAPTISM AND TEMPTATION.

AT last th' appointed hour has come ;
  Christ bows 'neath Jordan's swelling wave;
The mighty Baptist leads him forth
  Triumphant from that watery grave.

And from the heaven, serene and blue,
  While wondering souls with awe are stirred,
A dove-like form appears in view,
  Th' Eternal Father's voice is heard :
" Lo, this is my beloved Son —
The Prince of Peace, th' Anointed One ! "
O holy hour ! O sacred spot !
And yet, and yet, they knew him not.

And now the Spirit leads him far
  From busy haunts of life away,
Where gloomy shades of darkness are,
  'Mong fierce and angry beasts of prey ;
The Holy Spirit bids him go
To wrestle with the wily foe.

There, in that wilderness alone,
  With fainting form and pallid face,
Grievous temptations fierce and strong
  He suffers, for our fallen race.

But with the Spirit's mighty sword
  The prince of hell is put to flight ;

The strength of the Eternal Word
  Has conquered in Jehovah's might.

O tempted heart! when sorely tried
  Amid life's desert, drear and broad,
When hope and strength and courage fail,
  Look up, and put thy trust in God.

He will not fail thee; he who bore
  Temptations fierce and long for thee,
Who in the wilderness prevailed,
  Will give thee strength and victory.

THE MARRIAGE FEAST IN CANA.

(FIRST YEAR.)

THERE was a marriage feast in Galilee;
  The festal board was spread with viands
    rare;
The joyous guests had met in commune sweet,
  And he, the Man of Nazareth, was there.

Yes, he was there, that marriage, Eden-born,
  Might share the sanction of his presence
    sweet, •
That round this holy ritual he might throw
  A sacred halo, glorious and complete.

"The wine has failed;" the murmuring word
    is passed,
  And soon from lip to lip is borne to him;
Then sweeter far than music sounds his voice,
  "Fill ye these water vessels to the brim."

'Tis done: and wine, rare, purple, rich, and
        sweet,
    Th' astonished servants, smiling, bear away;
The while, methinks, the wondering guests
        repeat,
    "Ah, we have seen strange things —
        strange things to-day."

New, unfermented wine, the Master made,
    Not the mad wine that fills the drunkard's
        cup,
But such as he, the bridegroom, gives his
        guests
    Who at the marriage of the Lamb shall sup,
And drink it new within that kingdom fair —
His Father's glorious kingdom over there.

E'en thus it is along life's rugged path;
    Ofttimes it seems the wine of life is spent,
And we have nought to offer those we love
    But empty vessels, tears, and discontent.

O let us fill these empty vessels full
    With flowing sap, fresh from the living
        Vine ;
And we shall find, before the feast is done,
    That He has turned life's water into wine

CLEANSING THE TEMPLE.

AGAIN the Paschal feast had come,
    And strangers throng the busy street ;
While in the temple's sacred courts
    The buyer and the seller meet.
Shrill, babbling voices, wild and rude —
The shouting of the multitude ;
The lowing cattle from the fold,
The coo of doves, the clink of gold ;
The money-changer's greedy cry,—
Loud, eager voices, fierce and high,—
Discordant sounds from far and near
Are borne upon the startled ear.

"Take these things hence!" above the din
    There sounds a voice of stern command ;
The while, the awestruck throng behold
    A godlike Presence, firm and grand,
    With scourge of cords within his hand.

Then, like a mighty torrent rushed
    The surging mass, from pen and fold ;
The drivers with their cattle fled,
    The money-changers, with their gold ;
The screaming throng, the bellowing herds,
The bleating sheep, the frightened birds,—
All, all, in one vast, rushing tide,
From that stern Presence flee to hide.
In wild dismay they flee in fear,
As though th' Avenger's sword were near

THE WOMAN AT THE WELL.

THE sun rose high o'er Gerizim
And Ebal's mountains dark and grim,
As through Samaria's busy street
Echoed a woman's hurrying feet ;
The word is borne with bated breath,—
"Come see the Man of Nazareth,
By Jacob's well he sitteth now,
A holy radiance on his brow."

"He telleth of a fountain free,
Flowing for helpless souls like me ;
Of Christ, the Anointed Son of God ;
Of streams of mercy, free and broad ;
Of love and pity, hope and grace,
For the lost sons of Adam's race."

"Is not this he — the blessed Christ
Declared by holy men of old,—
The coming One, th' anointed King
Whom Moses and the seers fortold ?
Aye." quoth the woman, "Who may tell ?
Come, haste, he sitteth by the well."

They follow her — a multitude —
With eager haste and flying feet ;
And there, by Jacob's flowing well,
They listen to the message sweet :
"I am the living Fountain free ;
O thirsty soul, come unto me."

"Now we believe," they joyful cried ;
  " Yet not because of this thy word ;
For we with our own eyes have seen,
  With our own willing ears have heard !
And we will spread the news abroad
That Jesus is the Christ of God."

HEALING THE NOBLEMAN'S SON.

O'er old Capernaum the sun had set,
  And evening shadows gathered, dark
      and gray,
As silent watchers bent, with lashes wet,
  Above the cot where a frail sufferer lay.

The stars shone out like gems of purest light,
  And stormy Galilee was calm and mild ;
The calm blue waters kiss the wave-girt shore,
  And chant a requiem to the dying child.

"Father, come closer, closer to my bed,
  And let me lay in thine my fevered hand,
Before the vale of death my feet shall tread,
  Before I journey to that shadowy land."

"My child, strange rumors met my ear to-day ;
  For I have heard of Christ, the mighty One :
He tarrieth now by Cana's gates they say ;
  I go to seek him, that he heal my son."

He went ; his piteous plea the Master heard,
  As even now he hears faith's earnest cry ;
In tones of agony the father pleads,
  "O sir, come down before my son shall die ! "

Then, sweet as music, sounds the Master's
      voice, —
  Sweeter than birdsong in a desert drear :
"Thy prayer is heard ; O father, go thy way ;
  Thy little son shall live ; be of good cheer."

When from those sacred lips there falls the
      word,
  The pulse of health springs through that
      fevered frame ;
Soon old Capernaum the news has heard,
  And wondering souls believe on Jesus' name.

REPULSE AT NAZARETH.

He came unto his own, O shameful story!
His own received him not—the Prince of Glory.

THEY hated him ; and yet he came
 On love's sweet errand, down below,—
To lift the sons of Adam up.
To tell of life and joy and hope.
To drain for man the bitterest cup,
 And save him from eternal woe.

That he, the spotless Son of God,
 The Heir of Heaven's eternal throne,
Should count as loss all earthly fame,
For man should suffer woe and shame,
A blasted and dishonored name.
 And yet be hated by his own !

E'en Nazareth rejects his love !
 The home where he had long time dwelt,
And now he treads her streets once more,
Where he had led, in days of yore,
His spotless life, and o'er and o'er
 In humble prayer had knelt.

But they despise — reject him ! they
 To whom he brings the message sweet ;
They buffet him in angry strife,
And seek to take his sinless life ;
Seditious, cruel threats are rife,
 As scribes and rulers meet.

Yet, filled with mercy, o'er and o'er
  Those sacred hills and vales he trod,
Where spires from myriad cities gleamed
As Judah's sun upon them beamed,
And like one mighty city seemed
  From Lebanon's green sod.

To these, the pitying Master came,
  To bear his message from above ;
O Galilee ! thou sacred place ;
O Israel ! ye favored race ;
Why did'st thou turn away thy face,
  And spurn a Saviour's love ?

SERMON ON THE MOUNT.

O holy, sacred mount ! where sat.
  In human form, the Prince of Heaven ;
When, neath Judea's purple skies,
The sweet beatitudes were given:
Those gracious words, which echo still
Adown the corridors of time,
Till earth's remotest lands have heard
Their glorious symphony sublime.

"Blest are the poor in spirit,"— they
  Whose hearts are filled with godly fear ;
"And blessed they who mourn," for, lo,
  The heavenly Comforter is near.

Thrice blessed are the meek ; for they
    The promised earth made new shall tread :
" Blest they who thirst for righteousness,
    And hunger ; for they shall be fed."
" Blest are the merciful," and those
    Who gentle mercy's paths have trod ;
And sweet the benediction sure,—
    " The pure in heart shall see their God."

O blessed Peace ! How sweet thy sound
    'Mid noisy earth's discord and din !
Her restless sons of war and strife
    None but the peacemaker shall win.

And O, thrice blessed shall ye be
    If for the truth of God ye stand
When Persecution dark and dire
    Shall reach you with her bloody hand.

Rejoice and be exceeding glad ;
    The prophets suffered e'en like this,
And counted not their lives as dear
    Exchange for heaven's eternal bliss.

When wicked men shall falsely bring
    Dark accusations 'gainst your name,
And slander bold her banners fling,
    Truth's holy legions to defame ;
If thou, like Daniel, boldly face
    The king's command, the lion's paw,
If thou shalt conquer in the race
    And loyal prove to God's just law,
The King of Heaven shall be thy Lord,
Eternal bliss, thy sure reward !

THE DRAUGHT OF FISHES.

THE rising sun was scarcely seen
  Above Judea's hills so green,
And springtime flowers, bright and rare,
Dotted the landscape everywhere.

The gentle zephyrs, soft and free,
Ruffled the waves of Galilee ;
And where the morning sunbeams glanced,
Ten thousand diamonds gleamed and danced.

Already, o'er the cliffs along,
Wendeth an eager, anxious throng ;
The haughty priest, the man of care,
The lame, the halt, the blind, are there ;
For they have heard the joyous cry,—
"The MIGHTY HEALER PASSETH BY."

In Simon's boat the Master sat,
    And taught the people on the shore :
While scribes and elders stand amazed
    To hear such words of heavenly lore.
O Blessed Christ ! How vast thy love,
Unmeasured as the heights above !

"Simon, launch out into the deep ; "
    "Let down the nets into the sea ; "
"Yea, Master, at thy word we will,
    Though vainly we have toiled," said he.

The net is cast into the deep,
And quick within its meshes leap
The myriad fishes, small and great,
Until the sudden, mighty weight
Has filled the ships,—a cumbrous store,—
Till scarce the fishers reach the shore.

Then Simon bows upon the sod,
And worships him : "O Lord my God,
Depart from me ! for self and sin
Still gain the mastery within !"
And then, methinks, these words I hear :
"O Simon — wherefore dost thou fear ?"
"Let peace reign in thy heart again ;
From henceforth *thou shalt fish for men.*"

Ye wayworn sons of Adam's race,
O listen as these words of grace
Come rolling through the ages dim :
" *They left their nests, and followed Him.*"

"Come leave *your* nets, ye sons of men ;"
    These living words of sacred fire
Fall on our weary hearts again
    Like music from a heavenly lyre,—
Like chanting of the Seraphim :
"Come, leave *your* nets, and follow him."

HEALING THE IMPOTENT MAN
AT THE POOL.

WITH many a cry for pity,
  And many a weary moan,
Apart from the surging multitude,
  Sat the impotent man, alone.

Alone, by the Pool of Bethesda,
  Nor brother nor friend was near,
To plunge him into the healing fount.
  Or to whisper words of cheer.

His spirit was sad and weary,
  And his hope was almost dead,
And the smiling blue of Juda's sky
  Seemed brass above his head.

He lay where the sun at noontime,
  Was shining fierce and bright,
With never a shield from the heat by day
  Or the chilling dews of night.

And there he was waiting — waiting —
  With never a friendly word ;
Till his heart seemed dead like a broken reed
  With a hope so long deferred.

One day, as he sat by the porches
  Where the sick and the dying lay,
A gentle Form stood by his side
  And he heard a sweet voice say : —

"Would'st thou be healed, O sufferer?
    Arise, take up thy bed."
And he felt the thrill of a healing touch,—
    Of a soft hand on his head.

'Twas the word of the gentle Master
    That spoke to his weary soul,
His word that healed the impotent man,
    His touch that had made him whole.

O blessed, pitying Saviour!
    How vast is thy wondrous love!
'Tis deep as the depths of darkness,
    'Tis high as the heights above.

HEALING THE WITHERED HAND.

THE Sabbath — blessed guest — had come
    To visit old Capernaum;
Freighted with benedictions sweet,
With heavenly calm, and joys replete;
As when in Eden's new-born bowers
To Adam came its sacred hours;—
A loving Father's gift to man
When first the flight of time began.

Within that white-walled synagogue
    There gathered at the hour of prayer
A motley multitude; and He—
    The mighty Nazarene — was there.

They watched him, he, the sinless One,—
Th' Eternal Father's spotless Son ;
And would he heal th' afflicted soul,
And make that palsied sufferer whole,
On this, — the Sabbath ? hark ! methinks
I hear a voice of firm command,
Which heeds nor Scribe nor Pharisee :
" O man, stretch forth thy withered hand ! "

'Tis done ; faith grasps the promise sure ;
    The helpless, withered hand is healed ;
And once again, to human hearts
    The love of Jesus is revealed.

" Stretch forth *thy* hand," O fainting soul ;
    The blessed Master speaks to thee ;
He makes thy bruised spirit whole,
    And sweetly whispers, " Come to me."

" Stretch forth thy hand," the Lord will heal,
    Will calm thy tumult and thy strife,
Will bid thee quaff the Living Stream,
    And feed thee with the Bread of Life

RAISING THE WIDOW'S SON.

THERE was sorrow and grief, there was
anguish and pain,
In the humble abode of the widow of Nain,
And the hopes that once bright in her firma-
ment burned,
Like the "apples of Sodom" to ashes were
turned.

Her heart was bowed down by its burden of
care,
And her bright sun had sunk in the clouds
of despair;
Her light had gone out in the darkness of
night,
And her dreams of the morrow no longer
were bright;

For the Angel of Death, with his pinions so
gray,
Had taken the loved of her bosom away,
And the sorrowful women with wailings of
woe,
Were voicing the grief which they never could
know.

As out through the narrow gates of Nain
The solemn retinue gravely led,
The sunlight glimmered o'er hill and plain
And kissed the bier of the youthful dead

Look, over Esdraelon, there cometh a band
    That wendeth its way over valley and plain,
And now 'mong the mourners it silently stands
    As the dead is borne on through the gate-
    way of Nain.

Ah, see, 'tis the Master, the merciful One,
    Whose word has so oft brought the
    mourner relief ;
Will he pity that mother who weeps for
    her son,
And cheer her lone heart with its burden
    of grief?

Hark! richer than music that seraphims hear
    Is that voice, soft and sweet, that ascends
    to the skies,
As the Healer of Nazareth toucheth the bier,
    And biddeth the white-vestured sleeper,
    "arise!"

And the dull ear of death hears the life-
    giving word,
    And the strong chain of silence that fet-
    tered him breaks
As the black shades of death and of darkness
    are stirred
    By the voice of the Lord ; and the sleeper
    awakes.

O Jesus, my Master; how vast is thy love!
  I will sing of its depths while thou givest
    me breath,
'Tis high as the measureless heavens above,
  It is sweeter than life, and 'tis stronger than
    death.

STILLING THE TEMPEST.

JUDEA'S sun was sinking down
Behind Mount Tabor's hoary crown
The while, athwart the glimmering west,
The sunset shook her flaming crest,
And hill and dale and wood and lake
A magic beauty seemed to take.

And now far o'er the purple sea
Of changeful, restless Galilee,
I see, afar, a white-winged boat
Upon the billowy tide afloat ;
And sleeping on a pillow there,
I see a Form divinely fair.

Thus peacefully the moments fly ;
When, sudden o'er the purple sky,
Black clouds came up, and tongues of flame
From out the gathering darkness came,
And leaped, and blazed, and gleamed, and
    flashed,
The while the billows madly dashed,
And rolling thunder boomed and crashed.

From cloud-girt Hermon's snowy height,
The storm came down in sudden might;
And fiercer still the wild winds blew,
And black as night the storm cloud grew:
And louder still, and still more loud,
The thunder pealed from cloud to cloud.

And still, 'mid tempest-riven sky,
That white-winged vessel rideth high;
I see her struggling with the storm,
When lightning's flash reveals her form.
Hark! hear that cry above the roar
    Of howling wind and beating wave,
A hoarse voice calling o'er and o'er,
    "Master, we perish! wake and save!"

"What! hearst thou not the tempest's rage?
    How canst thou calmly lie asleep
When mighty waves like mountains rise
    To whelm us 'neath the surging deep?"
O Peter, Peter! knowest thou not
    'Tis He who formed the mighty sea,
Who holds the waters in his hand,
    That sleepeth now on Galilee?

The Sleeper wakes! he calmly speaks;
The wind and waves his words fulfill;
"Ye raging billows, cease your strife!
O howling tempest. Peace — be still."
'Tis done! the raging, wild winds ceased,
And evening breathed her breath of balm;

The rolling thunder died away,
And peace returned — there was a calm ;
And quiet nature sunk to rest
Like birdling in her leafy nest,
Or child upon its mother's breast.
O restless heart whose hope seems dead
　　When shadows rest o'er vale and hill,
When lightnings flash abvove thy head,
　　List, while He whispers, "*Peace — be still!*"

JAIRUS' DAUGHTER — "TALITHA CUMI."

SHE lay on her snowy pillow,
　　So silent and pale and cold,
And the summer sunshine flickered down,
　　And fell on her curls of gold ;
Till it seemed that a glorious halo
　　Had circled the dainty head,
And the heart of love could scarce believe
　　That the little maid was dead.

Jairus stands by the Master,
　　Trembling and sad and mute ;
For he hears the sound of the mourners' wail
　　And the dirge of the solemn flute ;
And the father knows that his darling
　　Has crossed to the other shore,
Where the "dull, cold ear of death" gives heed
　　To the voice of love no more.

"O why is this sound and tumult,"
  The pitying Master said,
' Why weep ye thus for the maid who sleeps,
  As ye weep for the silent dead?"

Then he spake to his three disciples,—
  To Peter and James and John,—
And the parents, sad, of the little maid,
  And they silently followed on,
Till they stood by the quiet bedside
  Where the waxen figure lay,
And they heard in the hush of the silent room,
  The great Physician say,
" *Talitha Cumi*,— Maiden,
  I say unto thee, arise!"
And the flickering breath of the child returns,
  And she opens her dreamy eyes.

There's a hush, like the calm that cometh
  In the solemn hour of night,
And a flush like the glow of morning fair,
  O'erspreadeth her brow so white.
There's a sigh like the gentle zephyr,
  At summer evening's close;
The thrill of a hand-clasp, strong and sweet,
  And the little maid arose!

O the love of the great Physician!
  The love that is strong to save!
I will trust in the Arm that is mightier far
  Than the chains of the dusty grave.

THE HEM OF HIS GARMENT.

WEARY and sick and fainting,
  Feeble and pale and wan,
Far over the hills of Gadara
  She wearily tottered on.

She had heard of the great Physician
  On the shores of Galilee ;
How he healed the sick and suffering,
  And made the blind to see.

And she said, "I will seek the Master ;
  Perchance he will hear my cry ;
I will seek this Jesus of Nazereth,
  I have heard that he passeth by."

Then slow, where the blue waves murmur
  Their sad and ceaseless song,
Along the cliffs of the Galilee
  There wended a mighty throng.

But ah, she is sick and fainting,
  And her step is slow and weak ;
And the bright tears spring to her eager eyes
  And drop on her pallid cheek.

She yearns for a look from the Master,
  For a touch of his healing hand ;
But the multitude surge about him,
  And throng o'er the wave-girt strand.

"I will touch the hem of his garment,"
    She murmurs in accents sweet ;
And she slowly creeps through the eager
        throng,
    And falls at the Master's feet.

And the Healer turns about him,
    And cries, "O trembling soul!
Thou art loosed from thine infirmity
    Thy FAITH hath made thee whole."

COMMISSION TO THE TWELVE.

TO be with Jesus — blessed thought !
    At early morn, at noon. at night,
To have his presence by my side,
    To lead my wayward steps aright, —
To hear his gentle voice, ah, this
It seems, had been exceeding bliss.

Ye chosen men, who by his side
    For three sweet years together walked,
Together roamed o'er Juda's hills —
    In loves communion fondly talked,
Ye knew Him! ah, how blest your lot,
When scribes and elders knew him not.

O chosen twelve : unknown and poor ;
  What mighty messengers are ye!
Your creed, Christ's blessed gospel sure —
  The gospel of sweet Liberty.
'Love as I've loved," the Master saith, —
"As high as heaven, as strong as death."

"Go preach my gospel ; heal the sick ;
  Go cheer the broken-hearted soul ;
Go set sin's weary captive free,
  And make each bruised spirit whole.
And unto you it shall be given
To sit upon twelve thrones in heaven."

FEEDING THE FIVE THOUSAND.

THE soft, spring day was nearly spent ;
  The hazy sun was sinking low,
As on that lonely desert place
  The multitude surged to and fro.

All day the mighty Nazarene
  Had calmed their sad hearts restless strife,
Had stilled their fears, and healed their sick,
  And fed them with the Bread of Life ;
And now the sun was almost set,
And still the people lingered yet.

"Come, send the multitude away,"
  O Master ; the disciples said,

"To-morrow is the Sabbath day,
  And lo, they faint for lack of bread "

And thus the pitying Master saith,
  In tender tones so soft and sweet,
While on the multitude he gazed,
  "My brethren, give ye them to eat.
They wander on the desert bare,
Like sheep without a shepherd's care.

"Yea, Master, yea, but how shall we
  With these few loaves and fishes, feed
This mighty throng, and scatter free
  To every soul as he hath need?"

What, knowest thou not that he—thy Lord—
  That mighty One who raised the dead,
And calmed the waves of Galilee,
  Can bring the famished people bread?

"Go, bid the multitude sit down."
  And there upon the waving green,
With awe-struck faces upward turned,
  A mighty multitude is seen.

With earnest eyes upraised to heaven,
  The pitying Master blessed and brake
The five small loaves and fishes two,
  And bade the multitude partake.

And they did eat, and went their way;
  And while their homeward paths they trod
Methinks I hear the people say,
  "*This Jesus is the Son of God.*"

LORD SAVE ME.

OVERHEAD the lightning flashes,
And the raging water dashes,
As upon the foaming sea
Of the stormy Galilee,
Peter and his comrades toil
While the angry waters boil.

Hark! the storm grows strong and stronger;
Can they keep their courage longer?
Look! a Form all clothed in white,
Fills their souls with dread affright,
'Till a well-known voice they hear
"It is I,—be of good cheer!"

Then they know it is the Master,
And their hearts beat fast and faster;
"Jesus, Master, speak to me;
Bid me—bid me come to thee,"
Speaks a voice in tones so brave
"Bid me walk upon the wave."

Thus the impetuous Peter crieth;
And the blessed Lord replyeth,
"Come;" and quick his hurrying feet
Tread the waves, his Lord to meet.
Ah! he sinks beneath the wave!
Jesus, O my Master! Save!

Then the Master quickly caught him,
Safely to the boat he brought him,

Whispering in his doubting ear,
"Wherefore, Peter, didst thou fear?"
Then the waves grow calm and still,
And the winds obey his will.

Ah, how oft, on life's rough waters,
Adam's faithless sons and daughters
Sink in sorrow and in grief,—
Sink in doubt and unbelief,—
Sink like Peter on the wave;
Till they cry "O Master, save!"

"Save me, save me e're I perish!
Vain are all the hopes I cherish;
Lead me, I am sick and sore;
Guide me till the journey's o'er;
Save me from the whelming wave;
Master, *I am sinking*,— SAVE!

Then the blessed Master hears them,
Strengthens and upholds and cheers them,
Gives them strength to do and dare,
Gives them grace the cross to bear,
Gives them courage all the way,
Till there dawns a brighter day.

Up! my soul, there's light and beauty
In the grand highway of duty;
Though like Peter ye may sink,
And the dregs of sorrow drink,
Though in danger and alarm,
Grasp the Everlasting Arm.

HEALING THE SYROPHENICIAN'S DAUGHTER.

TO the coasts of Tyre and Sidon,
　By the shore of the mighty sea,
The great Physician came one day
　From far-off Galilee.

And a Syrophenician woman
　Heard that he journeyed by,
And her loving mother-heart was stirred
　As she hears the joyous cry.

What joy, would he heal my daughter!
　I have heard he is good and kind,
That he gives to the deaf the hearing ear,
　And sight to the groping blind.

Will he hear a mother's pleadings
　For a poor, afflicted child?
What joy! if he calmed that troubled soul
　And banished the demons wild.

And her heart beat fast and faster,
　And the love-light in her eye
Told of a soul that was strong and true,
　Of a faith that could never die.

"O Jesus, thou Son of David,
  Have mercy on me, I pray ;
My daughter is vexed with demons wild,
  That madden her night and day."

"Come, send her away, O Master !"
  And the mighty Teacher said,
" It is not meet to cast to dogs
  The hungry childrens' bread."

" And yet the dogs, O Master,
  Of the childrens' crumbs may eat,
O give me a crumb from the Master's board,"
  And she fell at his blessed feet.

"How great is thy faith, O woman !"
  Though heaven and earth may fail,
In spite of the darkest fiends of hell,
  Shall the prayer of faith prevail.

And still, through the lapse of ages,
  The beautiful tale is told
How the Syrophenician's prayer prevailed,
  In the blessed days of old.

THE TRANSFIGURATION.

LIST, and I will tell the story
Of the Transfig'ration glory,
When the blessed Christ became
Glorified by fiery flame ;
And old Hermon's peak gave birth
To a radiance not of earth.

Could mine eyes have viewed that splendor,
Then my heart had grown more tender.
What ! could I asleep have been
Like those foolish, faithless men ? —
Sleeping while the angels trod
On that burning mount of God ?

Then, amid that flame supernal,
Comes the voice of the Eternal,
Echoing loud and louder still
Through each glory-glinted hill ;
And the distant snow-clad peaks
Tremble while Jehovah speaks.

And the while the three are listening,
Moses comes, with garments glistening,
And Elijah — man of God —
Hermon's sacred summit trod ;
And the mount, like flaming spire
Gleams and burns with dazzling fire.

Then speaks Peter, ardent, ever,
" Lord we need be parted never,

Here, three Succoths let us raise
For thy glory and thy praise.
It is good to bide us here,
Let us tarry, Master, dear."

But alas, alas for Peter!
Fades the vision fleet and fleeter,—
Fades the gleaming radiance bright,—
And the sable shades of night
Settle down where lately shone
Glory from the Eternal Throne.

And the three, so sad and lonely,
See no man save Jesus only,
But the glory all has fled
From around that sacred Head.
And poor Peter's hopes so fair
Vanish into empty air.

Ah, how oft some bliss elysian
Comes to us, like sweetest vision,—
Comes like Hermon's glory bright,
Comes — and fades in empty night.
Then may we, though sad and lonely,
See naught else save Jesus only.

DOOM PRONOUNCED ON THE IMPENITENT CITIES.

THE yellow sunlight flickered down
O'er hill and dale and busy town,
And autumn blew her fitful breath
About the Man of Nazareth,
As with his twelve he stood alone
  Upon the hilltops' purple crest,
While Galilee's bright billows shone,
  And Jordan bared her sluggish breast ;
While fair Magdala, calm and sweet,
Lay in her beauty, at their feet.

Afar to northward, rising high,
Capernaum's towers woo the sky ;
Bethsaida, in garments fair,
A thousand diamonds seems to wear,
As glorious day her banner flings
Athwart the Palace of the Kings.
From yonder dome the saintly priest,
  With silver trumpet loud and clear,
Proclaims in sweetly echoing notes
  That Sabbath's sacred hours are near.

But He, the Sabbath's mighty Lord,
  The Heir of the eternal throne,
Upon whose brow, on Hermon's height,
  Heaven's glorious radiance late has shown,
Him they reject, till now, at last,
Sweet mercy's blessed hour is past !

The Master speaks.   Too late! too late!
No power can turn aside thy fate.
With hands uplifted to the skies
The mighty Son of Mary cries.
" Woe unto thee Bethsaida,—
    Eternal and unending woe!
Had Tyre and Sidon seen these works
    They had repented long ago.

" Woe unto thee, Capernaum!
    Who wast exalted to the sky;
Thine hour is past, thy doom is fixed,
    Low in the dust thou, too, shalt lie.
Woe unto thee, Chorazin! woe!
    How oft hath gentle Mercy spread
Her blessed hands within thy streets!
    But now thine hour of grace is fled."

O careless one, and hast thou strayed?
    And dost thou mourn thy wretched fate?
Is sorrow's hand upon thee laid?
    And art thou poor and desolate?
COME, He invites thee, tempted heart;
    I list his gentle pleading still,
And ringing down the ages hear
    His blessed " WHOSOEVER WILL!"

THE TRIUMPHAL ENTRY.

FAR o'er the Mount of Olives' crest,
    The westering sun is sinking low,
As winding up the mountain side
    I see the joyous people go.

High over Hinnom's burning vale
    The Holy City gleamed and shone
'Mid shimmering gold and marble pale,
    Like orient queen upon her throne,
Till royal palace, dome, and spire
Seemed glowing with celestial fire.

And everywhere the shout is heard;
    Hosannas reach the very sky;
Vast throngs take up the joyous word,
    And answering echoes make reply : —

"O blessed is he that cometh, —
    That cometh in the name of the Lord ;
Hosanna in the highest ! hosanna !
    Come, echo the glorious word, —
Hosanna to the Son of David,
    That cometh in the name of the Lord !"

'Mid waving palms and victors' shout,
    'Mid songs of triumph rising high.
Loud hallelujahs glad ring out.
    And acclamations rend the sky.

While at the blessed Master's feet
    The royal city proudly lay,
In tender tones of pity sweet
    Methinks I hear him sadly say : —

"If thou had'st known in this thy day
   The things that to thy peace belong!
But thou hast filled, in haughty ease,
   Thy cup of violence and wrong!
How oft would I have gathered thee,
   Jerusalem, my chosen bride;
But thou hast turned thy back to me,
   In selfish vanity and pride;
And thou did'st cruelly condemn
   Thy Master, O Jerusalem!"

He weeps; as o'er that city fair
   He gazes with prophetic eye,
And sees upon her lordly walls
   The Roman banners proudly fly,
Her gilded domes grow dim with rust,
Her temple prostrate in the dust,
Her sons the screaming vulture's food,
And Zion's streets flow red with blood.

And well he knows that even they
   Who join the hallelujah cry,
Before another Sabbath-day
   Will madly echo, "Crucify!"

'Tis thus when life's ambrosial cup
   Seems brimming o'er with nectar sweet,
The world comes eagerly to sup,
   And casts her garlands at our feet.
But ah, when e'er life's cup is filled
   With gall and wormwood to the brim,
How oft we hear, with sad hearts chilled,
   The mocking cry,— "Away with him!"

THE CRUCIFIXION.

BEHOLD upon the shameful cross
  The spotless Victim dies.
' Mid cruel foes he yields his breath,
  A precious, priceless sacrifice.

The pitying sun withdraws his face,
  And shades of darkest night
Their black and dismal mantles throw
  Upon Mount Calvary's rugged height.

The flinty rocks are rent in twain !
  The graves give up their trust ;
And sleeping saints immortal rise
  Victorious from the silent dust.

Inanimate creation groans,
  And pitying angels weep !
And o'er the Master's lonely tomb
  Their solemn, sacred vigils keep.

O pitying Christ ! O Lamb of God !
  And did'st thou die for me ?
Then let my hand forget her skill
  If I forget thee, CALVARY

IT IS FINISHED.

'TIS finished all!   The fearful debt is paid!
    Now guilty man once more can lift his
    eyes,
And hope for mercy through the priceless
    blood
    Of Jesus Christ, the spotless Sacrifice.

'Tis finished all, and at the wondrous words
    Bright angels touch their golden harps,
    and raise
One grand, triumphant strain of victory;
    Thus tongues immortal shout in joyous
    praise.

O boundless mercy! depth of wondrous love!
    Fit theme for sages wise, or poet's song:
They lead the guiltless Son of God to die,—
    To suffer shame, and cruelty, and wrong.

O sinful man! how cans't thou e'er repay
    That love so deep, so infinite, so free?
Yield up to Him thy life, thy love, thine all,
    In grateful homage bow thy stubborn knee.

Go prove thy gratitude by deeds of love;
    Go wash thy spirit from its sinful stain;
Forsake thy pride, thy folly, that for thee
    The blood of Jesus be not shed in vain.

THE BURIAL OF CHRIST.

TAKE from the cross the dear form of the
    Master ;
Gently remove ye the nails from his hands;
Carefully cover the poor, mangled body,
    Loosen the cruel cords, sever the bands.

Take the rough crown from his pale, bleeding
    temple,
    Wash the dark stains from his dear, sacred
    head ;
Tearfully weep o'er the blessed Redeemer,
    Tenderly bathe ye the wounds of the Dead

Fold ye the hands that so often in kindness
    Healed, as by magic, the woes of mankind,
Ministered oft to the poor and the needy,
    Strengthened the sick and gave sight to the
    blind.

Fold ye them tenderly over his bosom,
    Over his loving heart, pulseless and still ;
Wrap ye his form, in the soft, pure linen,
    Tenderly bear him from Calvary's hill.

Tenderly bear him — the crucified Savior ;
    Lift from thy spirit its terrible gloom ;
Leave him to rest ; for the heavenly Watcher
    Waits but to call him to life, from the tomb

THE ASCENSION.

LIFT up your heads, ye glittering gates, —
  ·E'en lift them up, ye doors of pearl ;
The risen King of glory waits ;
  Let Heaven's banners wide unfurl !
Then voices cried, e'en like a roaring sea,
" Who can this King — this King of glory be ? "

Then from the bright angelic throng,
  ' Till heaven's myriad arches ring,
The glorious word is borne along,
  "The Lord of Hosts ! he is the King."
" Who can this King, — this mighty Con-
    querer be ? " —
"The eternal Prince of Heaven! tis he, tis he."

Lift up your heads, ye glittering bars !
  What glorious honors ye may win !
And brighter shine, ye heavenly stars,
  And let the King of glory in !
Ye everlasting portals, — open wide,
And bid thy risen King triumphant ride.

Asunder, 'mid a mighty shout,
  The massive, glittering portals rolled,
And hallelujahs glad rang out,
  As opened wide each gate of gold ;
Then with the mighty millions tried and true,
The conquering King of glory enters through.